A SLIVER OF MOON AND A SHARD OF TRUTH

STORIES FROM INDIA

CHITRA SOUNDAR

illustrated by UMA KRISHNASWAMY

**WALKER
BOOKS**

To my editor, Mara Bergman, for her love of stories from everywhere and a special thanks to Isaac for giving me the starting idea for this book.
C.S.

First published 2021 by Walker Books Ltd
87 Vauxhall Walk, London SE11 5HJ

2 4 6 8 10 9 7 5 3 1

Text © Chitra Soundar
Illustrations © Uma Krishnaswamy

The right of Chitra Soundar and Uma Krishnaswamy to be identified as author and illustrator respectively of this work has been asserted by them in accordance with the Copyright, Designs and Patents Act 1988

This book has been typeset in StempelSchneidler

Printed and bound by CPI Group (UK) Ltd, Croydon CR0 4YY

British Library Cataloguing in Publication Data:
a catalogue record for this book is available from the British Library

ISBN 978-1-4063-9813-7

www.walker.co.uk

A SLIVER OF MOON AND A SHARD OF TRUTH

STORIES FROM INDIA

Other titles by Chitra Soundar

A Dollop of Ghee and a Pot of Wisdom

A Jar of Pickles and a Pinch of Justice

Sona Sharma, Very Best Big Sister

CONTENTS

FESTIVALS ARE FUN

Long ago in a faraway land, King Bheema ruled a small kingdom called Himmatpur, surrounded by the magnificent hills of Himtuk. He was a kind and just ruler. He lived with his wife, Queen Tulsi, and his son, Prince Veera.

Prince Veera's best friend, Suku, was a farmer's son. He was neither rich nor royal. But he was clever, funny and brave.

Prince Veera and Suku often spent their days together studying or playing in the royal gardens.

For the last two summers, they had set up a court in the palace courtyard. They listened to people's petty problems and quarrels. Holding these court cases had taught them how to listen to both sides of a quarrel and decide who was right and who was wrong.

Everyone at the palace treated Suku just like a prince. But once, when Raja Apoorva had come to visit, he did not.

Raja Apoorva, the King of Peetalpur, was King Bheema's uncle. At first he had disapproved of the friendship between Prince Veera and Suku, a farmer's son. He also didn't like that Veera and Suku held their own court in the courtyard. But he later realized how well they worked together to solve tricky problems with wit and wisdom.

It was summer again and King Bheema had some exciting news for Prince Veera and Suku.

"Veera, Suku," said the king, "you have been invited to Peetalpur by Raja Apoorva to attend the summer festival. His daughter, Kanti, will also be visiting, with her little girl, Heera."

"Please could you check the letter again, Your Majesty?" asked Suku. "Are you sure I'm invited too?"

"Indeed you are," said King Bheema. "You both impressed my uncle during his last visit. Maybe he will even let you hear some cases in his court."

The boys were pleased. They loved solving problems.

Prince Veera and Suku set off on their horses early the next day. It took them from sunrise to sunset to reach the palace in Peetalpur.

"Welcome!" cried Raja Apoorva as he and Queen Parul came to receive them.

"Welcome, Veera," said Princess Kanti. "Welcome, Suku! I've heard a lot about the pair of you."

"Uh-oh!" said Prince Veera. "All good things, I hope."

"No crows to count here," said Raja Apoorva, referring to the case of the missing crows the boys had solved when he last visited Himmatpur.

"We're glad you've come to attend the festival," said Queen Parul.

"We can't wait," said Prince Veera.

"And thank you for having me too," said Suku.

"It will be spectacular," said Raja Apoorva. "There will be musical performances, wonderful foods to try, as well as painting, singing and martial arts competitions."

"That sounds exciting," said Prince Veera. "We can't wait!"

The next morning after breakfast, Princess Kanti and baby Heera accompanied Veera and Suku to the festival. When they arrived, the king was already at the festival grounds in the royal tent.

"Wonderful! You're just in time for the singing competition," and he led the way.

"Excellent," said Prince Veera.

The arena of the singing competition was unlike anything they had ever seen before. The stage was divided into two halves separated by a screen made of coconut thatch.

On one side was a peahen eating grain.

"Peahens don't sing," whispered Suku. "Why is it on the stage?"

"Shh!" said Veera. "It's starting."

One by one the singers came onto the stage and stood on the other side of the screen.

"What are they doing?" asked Prince Veera.

"Whoever makes the peahen sing back, wins,"

said Princess Kanti. "It's a new competition that one of our ministers came up with."

Soloists and duettists, some accompanied by musical instruments, and even a group of folk singers, all performed for the peahen. But the peahen took no notice – she was too busy eating grain. She called out only occasionally when the stage was empty.

"It looks like no one will win," said Raja Apoorva. "This is a tough competition."

"Veera," whispered Suku, "I think we can win this."

Prince Veera smiled. "Let me have a word with the king," he replied.

"Grand-uncle, maybe you will allow the two of us to compete?" he asked.

"Why not?" said Raja Apoorva. "The peahen wouldn't mind for sure."

Prince Veera and Suku walked onto the stage. "What should we sing?" asked Veera.

"Remember the time when we went to play near the fields and a peahen chased us?" said Suku. "We were saved by the call of the peacock."

Prince Veera smiled. "I see," he said. "So how do we call like a peacock?"

"Leave it with me," said Suku.

Prince Veera and Suku stood behind the thatch screen. "Ready?" hissed Veera.

Suku curled his lips and called out to the peahen in his best peacock impression. The call was sharp and long, just like the screech of a peacock. All those early morning peacock wake-up calls have come in handy, thought Suku.

The peahen lifted her head and called back.

Raja Apoorva rose from his seat and clapped.

Prince Veera and Suku had won! They danced with joy. But their happiness didn't last long. As the boys turned to leave the stage, the peahen tore through the thatch screen, looking for the peacock.

"Run!" cried Veera.

"I thought I found my calling!" shouted Suku as they both ran as fast as they could to the royal tent.

Raja Apoorva, Princess Kanti and baby Heera were already there.

"Let's proceed to the painting competition," the king said. "The peahen is no longer looking for you."

The painting competition was already underway.

Many artists were quietly painting as a drummer kept time.

"When the drummer stops, time's up," said Kanti, "and the competition is over."

"Why don't you two have a go?" asked Raja Apoorva. "Maybe you'll win this one too."

"B-but..." stammered Suku.

The drummer speeded up.

"That means there's less than fifteen minutes left," said Kanti.

"We can't compete this late," said Prince Veera. Some of the artists were painting beautiful scenes of the village and others were painting royal portraits. They were nearly finished by now.

"You two are clever and can do anything,"

said Raja Apoorva, with a wink. "At least that's what your father boasts in his letters."

Prince Veera and Suku looked at each other. They couldn't let King Bheema down.

"But we will try anyway," said Veera. "That's only fair."

"Fine!"

Suku picked up a pot of green paint, remembering the green pastures where peacocks roamed.

Prince Veera took the blue paint and brushed on blue skies above the green pastures.

The drum beats got faster.

"There's not much time left," whispered Suku.

Veera thought for a moment.

He grabbed a piece of charcoal and wrote "Cows Grazing Under a Summer Sky".

Suku frowned. Cows? There was no time to paint a herd of cows.

The drummer stopped. Time was up.

Raja Apoorva and Kanti went around to look at everyone's paintings. Soon they reached the easel in front of Prince Veera and Suku.

"Where are the cows?" asked Raja Apoorva.

Suku blinked.

Prince Veera smiled. "Your Majesty, the cows have grazed the pasture and moved on. You were a tad late."

"Where have they gone?" asked Raja Apoorva.

"To rest in the shade," said Suku, "to chew their cud."

Kanti laughed. The boys were indeed quick

with their thinking and with their paints, she thought.

Just then a soldier came hurrying up to the king. He spoke in a whisper.

"I was looking forward to the wrestling match at high noon," said Raja Apoorva. "But it looks like there's a problem. Let's go and see if we can fix it."

The boys followed the king, along with Princess Kanti and baby Heera, who was giggling and calling, "Moo!"

"Shh!" said Prince Veera. "We don't want a cow chasing us too."

The wrestling ring was under the hot sun. The ground was filled with sand. In the middle of the ring stood a wrestler thumping his chest. The crowd watched him impatiently.

"Who's ready to fight?" the wrestler shouted, jumping up and down.

The wrestler's muscles rippled in the sunshine like big waves crashing on rocks. Sand flew from the ring into the faces of the spectators every time he jumped.

"What seems to be the problem?" asked Veera.

"Do you see two wrestlers up there?" asked Raja Apoorva. "That is the problem. There is no one to compete."

Surely Peetalpur had many brave wrestlers, thought Veera.

The king was thinking the same thing.
He whispered to his minister, "Where are
Peetalpur's best wrestlers?"

"In hiding," said the minister. "No one wants
to fight this one. He is strong, mean and vicious.
He crushed someone's bones in the previous
match and it sounded like fireworks going off."

"Ouch!" said Raja Apoorva. "Still, our
kingdom's honour is at stake."

Suku nudged Prince Veera. "If only I were a
citizen of Peetalpur, I'd defeat this champion,"
he whispered and winked.

Prince Veera chuckled. "I don't think you
should say these things aloud, even as a joke."

But it was too late. Raja Apoorva had heard
what Suku said.

"Suku!" he called.

"Uh-oh!" said Prince Veera. "You're in trouble."

"So you think you can defeat the champion?" asked Raja Apoorva.

Prince Veera was worried. If Suku had to fight the wrestler, he'd be crunched like the crispy rice rings they ate at dinner the night before.

"But he's not from Peetalpur," said Prince Veera. "If he were a citizen of your kingdom, Your Majesty, he'd gladly defend its honour."

"That's easily fixed," said Raja Apoorva, taking the ceremonial sword from its sheath as Suku's eyes opened wide in fear.

"With the powers vested in me by the Almighty, I hereby proclaim that Suku is an honorary citizen of Peetalpur," said the king, touching Suku's head with the sword.

"What just happened?" blurted Suku. "Why did you get me into trouble?"

"I think what's about to happen is even more terrifying," said Prince Veera.

"You're now a citizen of our kingdom and you can fight for our honour," said Kanti.

"Grand-uncle, this is not a fight for boys," Prince Veera said. What would Father say? Suku's parents would not forgive him if something went wrong.

But Suku's honour was at risk and he wasn't going to back down. Yet how could he win this unfair fight? There must be another way to win, without fighting, he thought.

Then, as Prince Veera watched in horror, Suku jumped into the ring and sand flew up in a cloud.

The wrestler looked at Suku.

"This is the best that Peetalpur can offer?" he asked.

"There's no need to judge me before the fight," said Suku. "I don't even want to touch you in case I hurt you."

The champion wrestler broke into a laugh. "How will you fight without touching me? This is wrestling, my child, not hide-and-seek."

Some onlookers laughed. The king glared at them and they quickly quietened.

"I will wrestle you only if you qualify for the fight," said Suku.

"I don't need to qualify," said the wrestler. "I'm the reigning champion."

"So it'll be easy for you to qualify then!" taunted Suku.

"Are you afraid?" shouted Veera. "Shaking

like a leaf? Wriggling like a worm?"

The crowds cheered Suku on. The wrestler was put on the spot.

"Fine!" said the wrestler. "How do I qualify?"

"Whatever I do with my eyes closed," replied Suku, "I want you to do with your eyes open."

"And if I can do that?"

"Then we will wrestle," said Suku.

"Agreed," said the wrestler. How hard can it be? he thought. He was, after all, the champion wrestler across three kingdoms.

As the crowd chanted "Suku, Suku!" he closed his eyes. The champion watched. Suku bent down, picked up a fistful of sand and let it pour through his fingers and onto his face.

Prince Veera burst out laughing. Raja Apoorva slapped his thighs in joy as the wrestler looked aghast.

"Can you do this with your eyes open?" asked Suku, opening his eyes slowly.

"Only a fool would do that," said the wrestler.

"If you don't do it, you won't qualify," Suku reminded him.

The champion wrestler was clearly outwitted. He definitely didn't want sand poured into his open eyes! He jumped over the fence and stormed out of the festival grounds.

Peetalpur's honour was indeed restored.

"Well done, my friend," said Prince Veera. "I was so worried."

"Sometimes quick thinking is more important than brute strength," said Suku.

"You are indeed a true citizen," said

Raja Apoorva. "You're always welcome in my kingdom. Now name your reward."

"Food!" said Suku. "All that fighting has made me hungry."

FAMILIES DO QUARREL

Next morning, Prince Veera and Suku were invited to Raja Apoorva's court.

"PRINCE VEERA AND HONORARY CHAMPION CITIZEN SUKU!" called out the usher.

"Welcome to our court," said Raja Apoorva. Next to him was Princess Kanti and baby Heera, who stood up in her swan-shaped playpen and waved to them.

28

Ministers were seated on two sides of the room. Prince Veera and Suku were shown to their special seats.

"This morning we start with a puzzle," said Raja Apoorva.

"Oh no," muttered Veera.

"You think this is a test?" asked Suku.

"Everything is a test, my friend," said Prince Veera. "Respect has to be earned."

The king raised his hand to silence the two boys. "When I was on my morning stroll in the gardens, someone pulled my beard and moustache," he said. "They were also insisting on holding my hair and shaking it, laughing all the time."

The court gasped.

"What punishment does this person deserve?"

Ministers rushed to their feet in anger.

"How dare an intruder assault you!" said one.

"We must punish them with hard labour in the gardens," said another.

"Throw them in prison," said a third.

"Veera and Suku, what do you think?" asked Raja Apoorva.

Prince Veera smiled. "Wooden toys and a bag full of treats, Your Majesty," he said.

"Preposterous!" shouted a minister. "Your grand-nephew has no experience or sense."

Raja Apoorva wasn't upset at all. "Would you care to explain?" he asked.

Prince Veera smiled. "It's easy to deduce if you listened to the king carefully," he said. "Suku knows what I'm talking about."

Suku turned to the court and said, "If the king was strolling in his garden, surely only his family and the honorary champion citizen could go near him. Also if they dared approach the king and pull his beard, his guards would have stopped them, unless it was someone harmless. There is only one person who could reach the king's beard and moustache and hair."

Suku stopped and smiled at Princess Kanti.

"The king must have been holding his granddaughter in his arms," said Suku.

"And so we don't want to punish the 'intruder'," said Prince Veera. "Instead, she must be rewarded for making the king happy."

While the rest of the court was silent, Princess Kanti and Raja Apoorva clapped.

"Very good," Raja Apoorva said. "Veera and Suku, you are very perceptive."

"Veera!" said baby Heera, clapping.

"She can say your name," whispered Suku.

"Because it rhymes with Heera," replied Veera.

"I wonder if she can say 'honorary champion citizen'," whispered Suku.

After the puzzle had been solved, Princess Kanti excused herself and left the court with Heera.

"Please excuse my daughter," said the king. "She must oversee preparations to welcome her husband, my son-in-law, Prince Charak of Manickpur, who arrives today."

The boys spent the rest of the day in court, helping Raja Apoorva solve the problems of his people. Some came to ask for help, others to complain, just like in King Bheema's court. Raja Apoorva was fair and generous, though he did lose his temper from time to time.

Prince Charak was friendly and fun, just like Kanti. He played pranks, made Heera laugh and debated with Kanti on many topics – from

how to be a king
to how to roast
sweetcorn. Often
in the evenings,

he'd join everyone in the garden to play hide-
and-seek with Heera or play kabaddi with Veera
and Suku.

A few days later,
Prince Veera and Suku
were getting ready for the day.

"Prince Charak seems nice," said Suku.

"He does, doesn't he?" said Veera. "But that
doesn't mean I'll let him off easy when we
compete!"

Prince Veera, Prince Charak and Suku were
planning to meet in the palace grounds later that
morning for a friendly match of archery. Princess
Kanti and Heera were going to be the judges.

On their way, they met Raja Apoorva.

"Hello, Your Highness," said Suku. "Did you have a good morning?"

"No, and I'll have his head!"

Suku shook like a dandelion in the wind. Can honorary champion citizens be headless?

Prince Veera pulled Suku back.

"Your Majesty, you seem to be preoccupied," said Prince Veera.

The king glared.

Then Prince Veera bravely asked, "Can I help you with anything?"

"It's Prince Charak – I want his head!" bellowed the king.

"It won't fit *him*," whispered Suku, trying to suppress a giggle.

"Shh!" said Prince Veera, with a finger on

his lips. The king was famous for making hasty decisions when angry.

"Was there an incident, Your Majesty?" he asked the king.

"Prince Veera, you're the right man for the job," said Raja Apoorva. "Prince Charak has made my daughter cry. I want him imprisoned immediately."

Just then, Prince Charak came by. "Kanti won't talk to me now," he said. "I think she needs time to cool off."

Furious, the king came charging at Charak like a lion defending its den. Prince Veera and Suku pulled him back.

"Veera, arrest this man and throw him in prison."

"But, Sir," said Prince Charak. "Our discussion got heated and she misunderstood my words.

I'm sure she'll be fine later."

"That's it," said the king. "Veera, arrest all the sons-in-law in the kingdom and throw them in jail. They are all traitors who make our daughters cry."

Prince Veera looked at Suku and then back at the king. Just like Kanti, perhaps Raja Apoorva needed time to calm down too.

"Sir! Why me?" he asked, trying to stall.

"Because you are not yet a son-in-law," said the king. "It's my order and that's that."

Prince Veera sighed and turned towards Prince Charak. "Prince Charak, I'm arresting you for making Princess Kanti cry," he said. He took the prince by the arm. "Let's go."

Suku followed them, confused. "Veera, what are you doing?"

"You heard the king," said Veera. "We're

going to arrest all sons-in-law."

"But why are you pleased about that?" asked Suku.

"Because I have a plan to save Charak and all sons-in-law," said Veera. "But first we must hide Charak in my room."

Prince Charak rested in Prince Veera's room while Prince Veera and Suku hurried to the king's court.

Even though Prince Veera and Suku wanted to deal with the problem on their own, the news that all sons-in-law were going to be jailed had got out. Everyone was whispering. The king was nowhere to be seen.

"We must stop the panic before it turns into chaos," said Prince Veera.

He walked to the front of the court and signalled to Suku. Suku rang the gong by the door. A hush settled in the room.

"No one is going to be arrested and thrown into jail," said Prince Veera, "as long as you follow my advice."

"What do you know?" asked a minister. "You're just a boy."

"I'm not a son-in-law," said Prince Veera, "so I have the authority to arrest you if you are one."

The minister stopped talking.

"Listen up, folks," said Prince Veera. "The king is to be left alone today and not bothered by matters of state or people's problems.

If you value your life, you must obey."

"What happens then?" someone asked.

"Stay away from the king and by sunset the problem will go away. I promise," said Prince Veera.

The ministers shook their heads. They didn't have any confidence in Prince Veera.

"If you don't believe him, believe me," said Suku. "I won the championship wrestling competition, didn't I?"

Everyone smiled. "We trust you!" said a guard.

"That's settled then," said Suku.

Prince Veera smiled. Suku had indeed won the trust of the people. He was a true citizen of Peetalpur. "So what are you going to do?" he asked.

"I don't know," said Suku. "They trust me.

I trust you. So let's go and put your plan into action."

Over lunch, Prince Veera explained the plan to Suku and Prince Charak, who was still hiding out in Prince Veera's room.

"That's a dangerous plan," said Prince Charak.

"What if it backfires?" asked Suku.

"Let's hope for the best," said Prince Veera, "or we'll be joining the sons-in-law in prison."

Suku and Prince Charak waited in Prince Veera's room while Prince Veera approached the chief of the royal guards to accompany him to see the king. He was the only unmarried soldier in the entire palace.

"Didn't you ask us to lie low?" asked the chief.

"Not us," said Prince Veera. "No hiding for the brave and the unmarried."

Prince Veera knocked on Raja Apoorva's door.

"Who is it?" bellowed the king.

"Grand-uncle, it is I, Prince Veera."

"Have you arrested all the sons-in-law in the kingdom?" asked the king as he opened the door.

"Yes, Sir!" said Prince Veera. "I've arrested every one, except one."

"Who is it?" asked the king. "And what are you waiting for?"

Prince Veera stepped back. He straightened his shoulders and said in a clear, loud voice, "By the powers vested in me by the King of Peetalpur, I hereby arrest you."

"What are you talking about?"

"Chief, please take this man to prison," said Prince Veera.

 Raja Apoorva was furious. His moustache trembled and he rocked on his heels as his ears twitched.

"Sir, I'm just following orders," said Prince Veera. "And you gave that order."

"I didn't give an order to arrest me!" shouted the king. "Did your father put you up to this? Are you trying to steal my kingdom?"

Prince Veera stood his ground. "Your order was to arrest all sons-in-law," he said. "Therefore you must be arrested because you are a son-in-law too."

Queen Parul must have understood the plan. She took Veera's side.

"You were boasting about that order to me too," Queen Parul said.

"Yes, but ... but—" said the king.

"What's good for Charak is good for you," said Princess Kanti, standing next to her mother.

"But I did this for you," said Raja Apoorva.

"Did you even find out what they fought about?" asked Queen Parul. "Hasty elephants fall into the pit, didn't you know?"

"Father, it was a simple misunderstanding," said Princess Kanti. "We had a discussion, we argued, he said something, I said something back and it got heated. Charak and I talked about it this afternoon and we have sorted it out."

"And that's how fights must be resolved," said the queen. "Words not swords. I'm glad Kanti takes after me."

43

"One more thing, Father," said Kanti. "If there's ever a reason for me to raise the sword, I'm brave enough to fight my own battles."

Raja Apoorva smiled. "Yes, you are," he said. "You're brave and courageous and I overreacted a little bit."

"A little bit?" asked Prince Charak, who had come out of hiding with Suku.

Heera giggled and said, "Little bit."

"Fine, a lot," said Raja Apoorva. "But we were indeed lucky to have Prince Veera."

"We have one more thing to thank Veera for," said Princess Kanti.

"What is that?" asked her mother.

"Prince Veera and Suku have offered to entertain Heera while Charak and I go out for the day."

"That's not fair!" shouted Raja Apoorva.

Everyone stood still. Why was Raja Apoorva getting upset again?

"I want to look after my granddaughter," he said.

"Your Majesty, if I may," said Prince Veera. "Will you take us to the seaside? Suku and I would very much like to visit and we can help you look after Heera."

The next morning, as the rest of the palace and the kingdom of Peetalpur returned to normal life, Raja Apoorva and his guests travelled to the seaside in the royal carriage.

Heera loved sitting on her grandfather's lap and looking out at the countryside.

But soon the joy of travel wore off and Heera wanted to get down and play.

"Out!" she shouted.

"Not here, my child," said Raja Apoorva. "We're going to the seaside."

"Sea?" asked Heera. "Out!"

At first Suku tried to distract her with little games – what was hidden in his hand? Then Veera tried to point out the birds in the sky. But nothing worked.

Heera started to cry, "Ma!"

Raja Apoorva had been to battle. He had faced big problems in his court. But he didn't know what to do with a crying baby.

"I wish you could shorten this journey, Veera," he said.

"Maybe I can," replied Prince Veera.

Prince Veera clapped his hands and started to sing.

"On a horse by the tree, far away, by the sea, Heera went up and down, up and down, up and down."

Suku giggled. And so did Heera. Raja Apoorva moved his legs so Heera bounced on his lap, up and down.

"Again!" said Heera.

And they sang the same lines over and over again. For a long time.

"Raja Apoorva soon became bored of the same lines. "Maybe I can add a new stanza," he said.

"On an elephant in the shed…" he began.

The carriage stopped. The salty air and the roar of the sea greeted them. "Here we are!" announced Prince Veera.

"Oh no!" said Raja Apoorva. "How come we are at the seaside so soon?"

"You did ask Veera to shorten the journey, Your Majesty," said Suku, "and he has."

"Clever boys," said Raja Apoorva. "But I had a new stanza ready to sing."

"Make sure you remember the lines for the journey home, Grand-uncle," said Prince Veera.

"That's a good plan," said Raja Apoorva, getting down from the carriage with Heera.

As they made their way to the royal tent set up for them, the king thanked Prince Veera and Suku for handling the family quarrel and showing him how terrible short tempers can be.

"My father often says 'Return a punch with a hug'," said Veera. "Then there is nothing to fight about."

"Your father is a wise man," said Raja Apoorva.

"As a farmer's son, I can tell you, a king's haste causes a lot of trouble," said Suku. "When the king makes peace, the people are happy."

"Happy!" said Heera.

And they were happy at the seaside until it was time to go home.

NO FIGS FOR AN UNHOLY SAINT

A week had gone by. Prince Veera and Suku were enjoying their time at Peetalpur.

"Raja Apoorva is not all that bad once you get to know him," said Prince Veera.

"I agree, but I wish he would order more figs for the palace," said Suku.

Even though it was the season for figs, the basket in their room contained hardly any.

"Let's deal with the fruits later," said Prince Veera. "We've been invited to court.

Raja Apoorva is hearing people's cases."

Soon after Prince Veera and Suku took their seats at court, the king arrived with his usual fanfare. The drummers walked in front, beating out a drum roll. Then came the usher who announced Raja Apoorva's full title – "Raja Raja Mahaveera, Raja Apoorva arrives in court!" The ministers waited for the king to stride across the hall and be seated on his throne.

Soon the court settled into its routine. The king asked for updates about farming and the weather, the health of his people and the state of arts and culture in his kingdom.

Then it was time to hear cases. But the king had something else on his mind.

"Before we begin," said Raja Apoorva, "I need some information."

"Regarding what, Your Majesty?" said one of his ministers.

"The figs," answered the king.

Suku nudged Veera with his elbow. "He is a good king," he said. "The king of all figs."

"I knew you were going to ask about that," said the minister. "The fig seller is here with us today."

The guards brought in two men, Rustam and Dulal, walking far apart from each other.

"Figs and problems," said Suku. "Our kind of holiday."

"Veera and Suku," began the king, "I'm sure you're wondering why the king of the land should bother to worry about figs."

"Worry away," said Suku. "A good king

must always worry about figs."

Raja Apoorva chuckled. He seemed to be in a good mood.

"Let me tell you a story," he began. "Rustam, here, has a house by the river. One day when I was on my daily walk, a fig from Rustam's tree fell on my head."

"Did you punish him?" asked Suku.

Dulal sniggered.

"Of course not," said the king. "I praised him after I bit into the fig. It was the sweetest fig I had ever tasted. So since that day, all of the ripe figs from Rustam were sold to the palace," Raja Apoorva continued. "But this year, after a week, the figs stopped coming."

"That is a problem," said Suku. "Figs are essential fruits."

Prince Veera ignored Suku. "Why? Was there a problem with the tree?" he asked.

"That's what we're here to find out," said Raja Apoorva. "Tell us, Rustam, what seems to be the problem with the tree?"

"There is no problem with the tree, Your Highness," said Rustam. "My neighbour Dulal claims the figs belong to him and I can't sell them to the palace."

"How dare he!" shouted Raja Apoorva.

Prince Veera stood up. "Neighbours have tiffs all the time, Your Majesty," he said. "How is this a case for the king's court? Isn't this a private matter between you, Rustam and Dulal?"

"Anything that affects the king is a case for

the court," said Raja Apoorva's senior minister. "If the king is worried about figs, then he won't be able to focus on other things."

"Worry no more," said Veera. "We've dealt with neighbours who fought over water and neighbours who stole gems. Friendly neighbours are rarer than tasty figs."

"I love figs," said Suku. "We can help you with this case."

Raja Apoorva nodded. "Very well, I've seen you both solve tricky problems before. Sort this out and I'll make sure you get extra baskets of figs delivered to your rooms."

"Consider it done," said Suku.

He was already
dreaming about
the extra basket
of figs.

Prince Veera and Suku led Rustam towards the courtyard. Dulal was summoned too.

"We're back at our courtyard courtroom," said Suku.

"In a different kingdom," said Prince Veera.

"Now let's get some figs rolling," said Suku. "Rustam, explain why the figs stopped coming to the palace."

Rustam began his story. "I loved figs as a boy," he said. "When I was seven, I brought a cutting from my grandmother's garden and planted it in ours. Those days, all of the land belonged to us."

"Then what happened?" asked Veera.

"I looked after the sapling for years," said Rustam. "I used my free time to get the best manure from the cows in the village. I made sure the tree was pruned and well looked after."

"Then what happened?" asked Suku.

"One day my father sold some of our land to Dulal's family. They built a house on the land. But we never put a fence or wall between the two houses," said Rustam. "The tree was the marker. Everything beyond the tree was Dulal's land."

"I see," said Suku. "A fig of an idea is forming in my head."

"Did Dulal ever object to the tree?" asked Prince Veera.

"No, Sir," said Rustam. "The tree grew big and the figs it gave were sweet and tasty, just like the ones in my grandmother's garden. We shared the fruit with our neighbours too," he said, turning towards Dulal.

"Interesting," said Suku. "And when the king paid for the figs, someone saw gold coins hanging from the tree. Am I right?"

Rustam nodded. "This year, as the tree bore fruit, Dulal claimed that the tree belongs to him, so that he can have all the money."

How could the tree rightfully belong to Dulal? thought Prince Veera. For that he must hear Dulal's side of the story too. "Your turn, Dulal," said Prince Veera.

Dulal folded his arms in prayer to Prince Veera and said, "I've heard wonderful things about you, dear Prince. May your glory reach the farthest lands."

"Stop the buttering and start the uttering," said Suku.

"Just tell us why you stopped Rustam from sending the figs to the palace," said Prince Veera, smiling.

"I didn't stop him, Sir," said Dulal. "I wanted to send them to the king. After all, that tree has always been on our side. As good neighbours we have been letting Rustam look after it, climb on it and even eat the figs. But now that the king wants the fruit, rightfully the money should come to me and not Rustam."

"Is it true that the tree is on their side?" Prince Veera asked Rustam.

"The tree is the border, Your Highness," said Rustam. "We both get shade from the tree during the hot summers. Fruits fall on both sides when they ripen. The figs that the squirrels nibble and drop are the sweetest."

"It has been blocking my sunshine for decades now," said Dulal. "The squirrels are noisy and messy."

"But you're happy to be paid for the figs?" asked Suku.

"If the king declared the tree to be mine and would like to buy my fruit," said Dulal, "then of course I'll put up with the problems."

Now that Veera had heard both sides, he needed to verify their claims. Deciding right or wrong wasn't based just on instinct. It must be based on truth and facts.

"Take us to your house, Dulal," said Prince Veera. "The we can see the tree for ourselves."

Prince Veera and Suku rode to the village with the king's guards. On their way, they passed a temple. A holy man's portrait was placed outside the gates.

"I wonder who that is," said Suku.

"No time to think about that now," said Prince Veera, "we've a case to sort out. An important one at that."

Rustam's house was small, with a large garden around it. Dulal's house was big. But it had no garden. The fig tree stood between the two houses, spreading its branches wide.

The tree was laden with ripe figs, ready to be picked. The scent of the ripe figs made Suku's mouth water.

Prince Veera walked around the tree. He looked at the shade falling on both sides. Rustam waited quietly while Dulal paced in front of the prince. The tree was indeed in the middle of the two houses. It was Rustam's word against Dulal's whose tree it was. Veera and Suku needed a different plan to sort this out. They discussed it in hushed whispers.

"Right, we have decided," said Prince Veera. "All the ripe figs will be counted and divided between both of you. The king can pay you equally for them. Then the tree will be chopped up and you can each have half the wood."

"That's wonderful," said Dulal. "Great plan,

dear Prince. I'll even get my sunshine back."

"What do you think, Rustam?" asked Suku.

Rustam shook his head. Tears fell from his eyes. "Sir, the tree is innocent and precious," he said. "It's not the tree's fault that we can't agree. The squirrels that live off this tree, the bees that are in our gardens and, look, all those ants and sparrows feeding on the figs fallen on the ground – all those creatures will suffer."

"But we need to decide who owns it," said Prince Veera. "That's the only way to solve the problem. Otherwise the tree must go."

"There is another way, Your Majesty," said Rustam. "Dulal can keep the tree and sell the figs to the king every year. As long as he doesn't interfere with the animals and the fruit that falls on my side, he can take everything."

Suku gasped. "You will give up everything?"

"The tree is more important than the money," said Rustam. "I've looked after it since I was seven."

"That's settled then," said Prince Veera. "I hereby decree that the tree belongs to Rustam because he cares for it. If Dulal cannot be satisfied with the figs that fall on his side, then we will order him to leave this house and move to another part of the kingdom where there are no trees and no squirrels."

"Like the desert?" asked Suku, with a smile.

"But—" Dulal tried to speak.

Rustam thanked Prince Veera and Suku. "Thank you both for saving my tree. I'll make sure Dulal gets a basketful every season, if he wants one. And I'll bring the figs to the king before lunch."

With that settled, Prince Veera and Suku raced back to the palace to report back about the figs.

After lunch when the court was in session again, a little girl was brought before the King. She was accompanied by her parents. At the same time, the minister spoke to the king urgently.

Afterwards, Raja Apoorva said, "Prince Veera, can I ask you for your help again?"

"At your service, Your Highness," said Veera.

"Don't be hasty," said Suku. "What if he wants all our figs?"

"The minister wants me to look into a spate of burglaries in town," said Raja Apoorva. "Can you take the little girl and her parents outside and talk to them and try to resolve their problem?"

The little girl was crying. She was intimidated by the guards and the ministers.

"That's a wonderful idea, Your Majesty," said Prince Veera. "I'm sure she'd be more willing to talk outside the court."

Prince Veera and Suku asked the little girl and her parents to come to the garden with them. Princess Kanti was playing there with Heera.

"Hello," said Prince Veera. "My name is Veera. What's yours?"

The little girl smiled. "My name is Janvi," she said. "I'm six."

"I'm Nivas and this is my wife, Kamla," said Janvi's father.

Prince Veera turned to the parents. "Why are you here?"

Janvi's father hesitated, then said, "This might sound a bit silly."

"No problem is silly in the king's court," said Prince Veera.

"Last week we went to the temple for prayers and we saw holy man Sadhu Gul's portrait," Nivas said. "As more portraits appeared, spreading the word about his sermons, Janvi recognized him everywhere."

"Yes, we saw his portrait too," said Veera.

"What about it?"

Janvi's mother patted her  daughter on the head. "Each night we were leaving Janvi with my elderly aunt so we could go to the sermons. When we returned last night, we found out that my aunt's neighbour had been burgled."

"Oh, the burglaries Raja Apoorva mentioned," whispered Suku.

"But how's that connected to your daughter?" asked Veera.

Nivas wiped his face with his sleeve. "Sir," he hesitated.

Just then Janvi spoke up.

"It was a full moon last night," she said. "It was bright and shiny like my silver plate. So I was watching the moon through the window – and I saw Sadhu Gul."

"Did you see Sadhu Gul on the moon?" asked Veera.

"That's silly," said Janvi. "There is a woman on the moon, not a man. But from the window, I saw Sadhu Gul come out of the opposite house. He had a big bag in his hand."

"Maybe she thinks it's Sadhu Gul because she has seen his portrait all over town," said Kamla. "But what if it was true?"

"That's why we came to tell you," said Nivas.

"Maybe it is the holy man," asked Suku. "Maybe he slipped out of the temple."

Kanti was interested now. She came closer to listen.

"That is impossible," replied Nivas. "He was talking the whole time we were at the sermon."

"Did you actually see him there?" asked Kanti.

"No, not quite. But we heard him."

"What do you mean?" asked Suku.

"The holy man has been blessed with wisdom," said Nivas, "but not with vision. He is blind, so we all wear blindfolds when we listen to his sermons."

"So how does he go from town to town?" asked Veera.

"He has a trusted assistant," said Nivas. "The man who never talks. Some say he cannot speak."

"A blind sadhu and a silent assistant!" said Suku. "That's suspicious. What happened last night?"

"We listened to the sermon all through the

evening. We removed our blindfolds when the gong rang. Sadhu Gul was seated right in front of us."

If Nivas was right and Sadhu Gul spoke all night, how did Janvi see him rob the house? So was the holy man blind or not?

"We need to figure out if this man is really holy or if this is all just jaadoo joli," said Suku.

"You suspect magic tricks?"

"I suspect tricks, maybe not magic," said Suku. "I have a plan, but it involves the king and I'd like you both to request his cooperation."

"What? The honorary champion citizen is afraid of the king?" teased Kanti.

"Courage is knowing how not to get into trouble," said Suku. "Why don't you and Veera ask the king?"

"Ask what?" said Prince Veera. "Do you want to tell us what the plan is?"

Suku huddled with Veera and Kanti to explain his plan to expose the holy man who might be the burglar.

"That may just work," said Prince Veera.

"It'll be fun to catch a burglar," said Kanti. "Thank you for including me in your plan."

"Catch!" said Heera, running inside. Kanti laughed and followed her, along with Prince Veera, to the king's chambers.

"Sadhu Gul is very famous and the people love to hear him speak, Your Highness," said Prince Veera. "I think we should host him at the palace."

"But I'm too busy," said Raja Apoorva.

"Father, people will thank you for it," said Princess Kanti. "Listening to sermons enhances our culture."

"And we will take care of the arrangements," said Prince Veera. "Just come for an hour at sunset to start us off. You won't have to stay long."

"Fine," said Raja Apoorva. "How could I say no to my favourite daughter?"

"I'm your only daughter," said Kanti, and chuckled.

Everyone in the town was invited to the palace for the sermon. When they arrived, each was given a black cloth as a blindfold. The holy man came in holding the hand of his assistant, who guided him through to the front of the hall.

Prince Veera and Princess Kanti were dressed in their royal attire – from crown to sword.

"I prefer the sword to the crown," said Kanti.

"I agree with you," said Veera.

Suku smiled. "No crowns or swords for farmers," he said. "But today's plan relies on

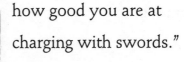 how good you are at charging with swords."

Kanti nodded hesitantly.

"Something bothering you, Princess Kanti?" asked Prince Veera.

"What if Sadhu Gul really is a blind saint and our plan backfires?"

"Then even our swords won't save us from your father's wrath," said Prince Veera.

"Look at it this way," said Suku. "If this holy man is pretending to be blind and his assistant is pretending he can't speak, no one will know who to trust. People may think others are pretending too. We must take this risk."

"That's true," said Kanti. "Let's hope our plan works."

As everyone settled into their seats, the king arrived with his ministers.

Once everyone was blindfolded, the sermon began. Sadhu Gul's voice rang through the silent hall.

Prince Veera and Princess Kanti stood by the door facing Sadhu Gul. Suku stood next to Prince Veera near the gong. As the holy man launched into a hymn, Prince Veera and Princess Kanti clinked their swords together. It was time. Suku rang the gong.

All the people assembled in the hall, including the king, removed their blindfolds to see what was going on. The holy man's eyes fluttered open as if he had come out of a trance. His assistant took a few steps back.

"Now," whispered Suku. Princess Kanti and Prince Veera charged towards Sadhu Gul with their swords raised.

In a flash, without any help from his assistant, Sadhu Gul jumped from his seat and ran through the crowd towards the palace gates. The assistant ran towards the back door that led to the garden.

"Catch them both and bring them here!" ordered Prince Veera.

"Veera, Kanti," said Raja Apoorva. "What is going on? I thought you wanted to listen to the sermon. Why did you attack the blind man?"

"Blind man?" asked Suku. "He shot out of the door before you could say honorary champion citizen."

Sadhu Gul and his assistant were summoned before the king and all the people who had gathered there. And the two men confessed everything about the burglaries.

"While everyone was blindfolded and sat through the sermons, I went into their houses to burgle," admitted Sadhu Gul.

"But what about the sermons?" asked the king.

"My assistant mimicked my voice and gave the sermons," said Sadhu Gul.

"He's a performer I had hired to help me with my plan."

Raja Apoorva gestured for them to be taken away. "Lock them up," he said, and turned to Prince Veera and Suku. "How did you even suspect the holy man?" he asked.

Prince Veera looked at Suku. "It was all Suku's instinct and plan," he said.

"Janvi had no reason to lie or make things up," said Suku. "I believed her. She did see Sadhu Gul with the bag."

Then he congratulated them on not just solving the burglaries in the capital but also across the kingdom. The sadhu had been busy.

"Your plan worked," said Princess Kanti, after everyone had gone home.

"Put your trust in me," said Suku. "You'll only see victories."

Everyone laughed as they sat down under the moonlight while Suku pretended to make the figs disappear.

"I'll trust you with my life," said Prince Veera, "but never with the figs."

AN IMPROBABLE DREAM

Prince Veera and Suku had spent two weeks at Peetalpur. Their visit was nearly over.

"I'm looking forward to going home," said Prince Veera. "There's just one more thing left to do here."

Before Suku could find out what that was, it was time to join Raja Apoorva for breakfast in the royal garden. Baby Heera was playing with the gardener and the king was strolling on the garden path.

"Good day to you, Your Highness," greeted Prince Veera.

"Good day to you both," replied the king. "I've some news for you."

The king put an arm around Prince Veera and they started walking. Suku followed right behind.

"I understand you have a keen interest in astronomy," said Raja Apoorva. "My ministers tell me that the famous astronomer Ehsan Atari is spending some time at Peetalpur and will be joining us for dinner tonight."

Prince Veera smiled. "Wonderful!" he said. "I was about to ask you about that. I was just telling Suku I have one more thing to do before we leave."

They strolled the length of the long path, from the rose garden to the rock garden, then Prince Veera and Suku stopped to play with Heera.

"Again!" she shouted.

The king turned to see Veera and Suku somersault three times in a row, making Heera laugh. But the king didn't watch where he was going. He tripped on a stone and fell.

The gardener gasped and rushed to the king's side. Prince Veera and Suku came over to help. But baby Heera thought the king was trying to make her laugh too. She laughed and demanded, "Again."

This made everyone smile – except the king.

"Isn't it your job to keep the path clear of stones?" he asked the gardener.

The gardener didn't know what to say. They were not standing on the path. The king had strayed into the rock garden.

"You caused me to fall!" shouted the king, embarrassed. "This is treason."

"But, Sir," began the gardener, "I didn't wish you to fall. My family has worked for you for generations. I've never wished to harm you."

But Raja Apoorva was still hearing Heera's laugh and seeing the smiles of amusement on everyone's faces. As well as being embarrassed, he was now upset.

"I know you've been loyal," said the king, not wanting to back down. "That's why I'm not throwing you in prison. I want you to leave the kingdom by sunset."

The gardener turned away and walked back to his cottage in silence. Suku nudged Prince Veera but Veera knew that this was not the time to argue with Raja Apoorva. Suku held baby Heera and they proceeded to breakfast.

After breakfast, Prince Veera went to see the gardener. The gardener was devastated.

"You must be angry and upset with the king," said Prince Veera.

"I'm not angry, dear Prince," said the gardener. "I'm just worried for the king."

"Why?" asked Prince Veera.

"I don't want anyone to speak ill of him," said the gardener. "Tongues will wag, people will talk about how unfair Raja Apoorva is."

Prince Veera was touched by the gardener's loyalty. I must do something, he thought.

"Can I ask you one last thing before you go?" asked Prince Veera. "It will save the king's reputation."

"Anything for my king," said the gardener.

Back in the palace, Suku was trying on new tunics for the dinner. Prince Veera was helping him decide.

"What do you think of this one, Veera?" asked Suku, turning around to show off a red tunic.

"Wear something simple," answered Prince Veera. "We're meeting an astronomer, not a princess."

"Easy for you to say," said Suku. "Whatever you wear, you'll be a prince."

As Suku tried to make up his mind, Prince Veera told Suku about the gardener and his plan to save his job.

"Will it work?" asked Suku. "The king has a very short temper."

"And a big heart," said Veera. "Sometimes you have to dig up the garden to plant some roses."

"Did you learn that from the gardener too?" asked Suku, laughing.

After lunch, the boys spent the afternoon packing. They had so many gifts to carry back home, including the baskets of figs.

Prince Veera told Suku how excited he was about meeting the astronomer Ehsan Atari. He had written a list of questions about the comets, the stars and the moon.

"If you keep asking him questions, when will

the astronomer eat?" asked Suku. "You do realize that he's expecting to eat at the dinner?"

"Fine! I'll ask the questions before and after the meal," said Veera. "It might be a long night."

At sunset, Prince Veera and Suku entered the royal banquet hall. Prince Veera's smile evaporated when he entered.

"What's this?" Suku whispered.

In front of them were twelve men – six on each side of Raja Apoorva. They all looked identical. They wore the same clothes and the same turban and they all had the same beard.

"Welcome, Prince Veera and Honourable Champion Citizen Suku," said Raja Apoorva. "Your esteemed guest, Ehsan Atari, is here. He is one of the twelve men. If you can find him, you can have dinner with him."

"Oh no!" said Suku. "I should have eaten before we arrived."

"Don't worry, I know how to find Ehsan Atari," said Prince Veera. He took a few steps forward. "Everyone seems so tense, Your Highness. Perhaps I should tell a story."

The king nodded.

"After packing for my return journey home, I took a nap this afternoon," began the prince.

"Did you?" whispered Suku. "When?"

"During my nap, I had a dream," Veera continued, ignoring Suku. "In that dream, Raja Apoorva and I were walking in the garden."

Suku did not like where this was going. The garden was not the king's favourite topic of the day.

The twelve men and Raja Apoorva listened closely.

"As we were walking, we tripped on a stone," said Prince Veera.

Suku was even more worried. The king didn't like falling down. Didn't they see how he reacted that morning? Veera was asking for trouble.

Veera continued. "In my dream, the weirdest thing happened. The king fell into a ditch full of honey."

Raja Apoorva shouted, "Hang on!"

"Hang on to your head," whispered Suku.

"The king might cut it off at any time now."

"I had the same dream," said the king. "How strange is that? In my dream I did fall into a ditch full of honey. But Veera, here, fell into a ditch full of mud."

"Uh-oh!" said Suku.

"That's right, Your Highness," said Prince Veera, thinking quickly. "When we came out, we were captured by an enemy general who demanded we clean each other up. I had to lick the honey off your hands and you had to lick the mud off mine."

As soon as Prince Veera finished, the third man to the king's right laughed aloud. None of the others did. Even Suku wasn't brave enough to laugh.

Prince Veera walked up to the man who laughed and said, "Thank you for coming,

Ehsan Atari. I have so many questions to ask you."

Raja Apoorva clapped his hands in approval. "Well done, Veera!" he said. "How did you know?"

Prince Veera turned to face the king. "Eleven of the people here work for you," said Prince Veera. "They must have heard about what happened to the gardener. So none of them dared to laugh in front of you."

Suku nodded with a smile.

"But Ehsan Atari is a travelling astronomer," continued Prince Veera. "He doesn't work for anyone and so he dared to laugh."

"I follow the moon and the stars," said Ehsan Atari, "not orders."

Raja Apoorva smiled and Suku sighed.

Now we can eat, thought Suku. And they did.

Ehsan Atari and Prince Veera discussed the planets, the comets, the stars and the moon for a long time. At the end of the meal, Prince Veera invited Ehsan Atari to visit King Bheema's palace at Himmatpur.

"That will be my pleasure," said the astronomer.

As everyone left the banquet hall, they heard voices.

The king turned to see the gardener rush through the doors.

"What are you doing here?" asked the king.

"Didn't I order you to leave?"

The gardener looked at Prince Veera, who nodded. The gardener fell at the king's feet and spat on the king's shoes.

"How dare you!" yelled the king. "Guards! Capture this disrespectful man and throw him in prison."

Prince Veera said, "Your Highness, if I may."

"No! You may not!" the king snapped.

"Please ask him, Sir," continued Prince Veera, without fear, "why he would do such a thing. Why would he do this when he could have left the kingdom and easily found a job somewhere else?"

The king looked at the gardener and nodded.

The gardener broke down in tears. "Sir, when you banished me because you tripped over the rock, everyone talked about how unfair it was."

He explained. "They spoke ill of you, so I wanted to give them a good reason. Now they'll say my punishment is well deserved and your good name will not be tarnished."

The king ran to the gardener and hugged him. "I realize now that I was unfair. I was embarrassed to fall over in front of my precious granddaughter and I took it out on you. I'm sorry. Forgive me for my haste."

The gardener cried in gratitude. It was generous of the king to apologize to his gardener.

"Go back home and return to work as normal tomorrow," added the king. As the gardener left the hall, Raja Apoorva put his arm around Prince Veera.

"Thank you for bravely helping the gardener," said the king.

"Perhaps we can celebrate with some somersaults for baby Heera inside the palace?" asked Suku.

"I'm too old for that," said Raja Apoorva. "I'll have you do it."

"If you please, not after this sumptuous dinner, Your Highness," said Suku.

That night Prince Veera lay down on his bed and watched the crescent moon from his window. What should he say in his farewell words to Raja Apoorva and his family? Those would be the final things the king would remember him by, until they met again. He must praise the king and yet...

Next day, Raja Apoorva and his family had gathered at the palace gates to bid farewell to Prince Veera and Suku. The king had added two more carts full of presents to accompany them. Suku walked around them one last time.

"Come on," called Prince Veera. "It's time to leave."

"I'm just checking that the figs haven't been forgotten," said Suku.

Princess Kanti and baby Heera came over to say goodbye.

"I'm going to miss Heera," said Suku.

"You have Veera, I have Heera," said Princess Kanti.

Baby Heera giggled.

"Have a safe journey," said Princess Kanti.

"We'll miss you in the palace," said Queen Parul.

"Thank you for making us feel so welcome," said Prince Veera. "We've had a wonderful time."

"Thank you," said Suku. "I'll be back, because I'm an honourable champion citizen now."

"Yes, you are, Suku," said Raja Apoorva. "You must visit again. Perhaps with your parents?"

"Thank you, Your Highness," said Suku.

Then it was time for Veera to formally bid farewell to Raja Apoorva.

"Thank you, Grand-uncle," said Prince Veera. "We loved our time here and enjoyed listening to some of your cases, participating in the summer festival and going to the seaside. You're a full moon in splendour compared to our own glory in the waxing crescent."

"You're welcome," said Raja Apoorva. "May you live long and prosper."

After taking leave, Prince Veera and Suku mounted their horses, followed by an entourage of carts. They sped through the villages and towns, crossed the river and reached home just after sunset.

King Bheema and Queen Tulsi were waiting at the palace gates. Suku's parents had come too. Prince Veera and Suku brought their horses to a halt just as they approached the palace. They jumped down to be greeted, to fanfare and music, drums beating and horns blaring.

"Thank you!" shouted Prince Veera. "Thank you for this warm welcome."

"What?" shouted King Bheema. "I can't hear you."

"It's a loud welcome," said Suku, raising his hand to stop the music.

"Was your journey pleasant?" asked Queen Tulsi.

"Yes, it was," said Prince Veera. "We raced against each other most of the time."

Then they made their way into the palace and straight to the dining hall.

"Suku's mother insisted on cooking at the palace today," said King Bheema.

"That's the best welcome present ever!" said Suku.

"My stomach and I couldn't agree more," said Prince Veera.

Suku's mother had prepared all their favourites – lentil pancakes with peanut chutney and tangy tamarind rice. There was a side of mango pickles, and dessert was coconut and almond burfis.

As they ate, Veera and Suku alternated telling stories about their stay at Peetalpur.

"How about some of those legendary figs?"

asked King Bheema after Suku explained how they had saved the tree.

"Just a couple for each of you," said Suku, handing out sweet figs to everyone. "The rest are all ours."

"A greedy stomach runs fast," Suku's mother warned him.

"I'm joking," said Suku, winking at Veera. "Surely I wasn't going to eat all the figs."

"So it all went well then," asked King Bheema, biting into a sweet fig. "I was worried that Raja Apoorva's temper would cause trouble."

"None that we couldn't fix," said Prince Veera.

"Except one thing though," said Suku.

Everyone turned to Suku. Did anything untoward happen?

"It's just something I've been thinking about since we set off from Peetalpur," said Suku. "Veera said, 'You're a full moon in splendour compared to our own glory of the waxing crescent'."

"What's wrong with that?" asked Prince Veera.

"Why were you so humble before him?" asked King Bheema. "You called him a full moon. Our kingdom is larger and more prosperous than Peetalpur."

"First of all, he is your uncle," said Prince Veera. "My farewell greeting must be respectful. But I wasn't being humble at all. Think about it."

Suku put down the fig he was eating and closed his eyes. Then suddenly he jumped up. "I got it!" he cried.

"What?" asked King Bheema

"A full moon has already reached its potential," said Suku, "whereas a waxing crescent will grow into a full moon. The best is yet to come."

"That's right," said Prince Veera. "I wanted to wish him farewell in a way he wouldn't be offended by and without having to humble myself."

"That's shrewd," said King Bheema.

"Let's hope Raja Apoorva doesn't work it out," said Suku, giggling.

Later that night, as the adults retired to their rooms, Prince Veera and Suku watched the waxing moon quietly. They were happy to be home again.

AUTHOR'S NOTE

As a child growing up in India, my favourite stories were trickster tales. They still are. I listened to stories about Tenali Rama, Birbal and Emperor Akbar and so many more in the same folklore traditions of India, and a big dose of Mullah Nasruddin stories from Persia. These stories stayed with me as I became an oral storyteller and writer.

I reimagined these folk stories as adventures of Prince Veera and Suku, while staying true to the spine and wisdom of the ancient tales. In the tradition of folklore, I've passed these on to new readers and listeners. The attire of the stories might have changed, but their fabric remains timeless.

I hope you enjoy reading these stories and that you will pass them on to your friends and family.

Chitra Soundar
Author and storyteller

CHITRA SOUNDAR is originally from the culturally colourful India, where traditions, festivals and mythology are a way of life. As a child, she feasted on generous portions of folktales and stories from Hindu mythology. As she grew older, she started making up her own stories. Chitra now lives in London, cramming her little flat with storybooks of all kinds.

UMA KRISHNASWAMY enjoys art in all its various flavours, classical to folk to naive to outsider art. These age-old and contemporary traditions are a wish-fulfilling tree in terms of inspiration for her artistic experiments. She lives and teaches at various art colleges and schools in Chennai, where she gets to combine two great passions, art and history.

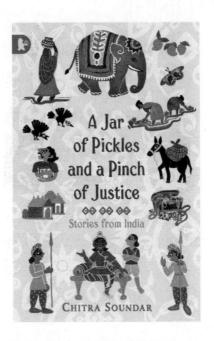

A Jar of Pickles and a Pinch of Justice

Stories from India

CHITRA SOUNDAR

Come and meet a greedy group of pickle-swapping, crow-culling, revenge-seeking crooks! A jealous potter, a nasty guest, five fools ... and more!

Prince Veera, with the help of his best friend, Suku, returns to settle the problems in his father's court.

When Sona Sharma learns she is to become
a big sister, she is determined to think up
the perfect name for her new sibling. Sona
may not be sure about sharing her beloved
family, but she definitely wants to be the very
best sister she can be.

*"Told with warmth, humour and detail to ritual that
will bring smiles of recognition across generations."*
Sita Brahmachari